A
LONG WALK
TO
WATER

Map of Sudan, 1985

A LONG WALK TO WATER

A novel by

LINDA SUE PARK

BASED ON A TRUE STORY

Houghton Mifflin Harcourt
Boston | New York

Originally published in hardcover in the United States by Clarion Books,
an imprint of Houghton Mifflin Harcourt Publishing Company, 2010.

For information about permission to reproduce selections from this book, write to
trade.permissions@hmhco.com or to Permissions, Houghton Mifflin Harcourt
Publishing Company, 3 Park Avenue, 19th Floor, New York, New York 10016.

www.hmhco.com

The text of this book is set in 11.5-point Celestia Antiqua
and 12-point Le Havre Rounded Light.

Map illustration by Kayley LeFaiver.

LIBRARY OF CONGRESS CATALOGING-IN-PUBLICATION DATA
Park, Linda Sue.
A long walk to water : based on a true story / by Linda Sue Park.
p. cm.
Summary: When the Sudanese civil war reaches his village in 1985, eleven-year-old
Salva becomes separated from his family and must walk with other Dinka tribe
members through southern Sudan, Ethiopia, and Kenya in search of safe haven. Based
on the life of Salva Dut, who, after emigrating to America in 1996, began a project to
dig water wells in Sudan.
I. Dut, Salva, 1974?—Juvenile fiction. [1. Dut, Salva, 1974?—Juvenile fiction. 2.
Refugees—Fiction. 3. Survival—Fiction. 4. Water—Fiction. 5. Blacks—Sudan—Fiction.
6. Sudan—History—Civil War, 1983–2005—Fiction.] I. Title.
PZ7.P22115Lo 2009
[Fic]—dc22
2009048857

ISBN: 978-0-547-25127-1 hardcover
ISBN: 978-0-547-57731-9 paperback

Manufactured in the United States of America
DOC 40 39 38 37 36

4500693410

To Ben, again

CHAPTER ONE

Southern Sudan, 2008

Going was easy.

Going, the big plastic container held only air. Tall for her eleven years, Nya could switch the handle from one hand to the other, swing the container by her side, or cradle it in both arms. She could even drag it behind her, bumping it against the ground and raising a tiny cloud of dust with each step.

There was little weight, going. There was only heat, the sun already baking the air, even though it was long before noon. It would take her half the morning if she didn't stop on the way.

Heat. Time. And thorns.

Southern Sudan, 1985

Salva sat cross-legged on the bench. He kept his head turned toward the front, hands folded, back perfectly straight. Everything about him was paying attention to the teacher—everything except his eyes and his mind.

His eyes kept flicking toward the window, through which he could see the road. The road home. Just a little while longer—a few minutes more—and he would be walking on that road.

The teacher droned on with the lesson, about the Arabic language. Salva spoke the language of his Dinka tribe at home. But in school he learned Arabic, the official language of the Sudanese government far away to the north. Eleven years old on his last birthday, Salva was a good student. He already knew the lesson, which was why he was letting his mind wander down the road ahead of his body.

Salva was well aware of how lucky he was to be able to go to school. He could not attend the entire year, because during the dry season his family moved away from their village. But during the rainy season, he could walk to the school, which was only half an hour from his home.

Salva's father was a successful man. He owned many head of cattle and worked as their village's judge—an honored, respected position. Salva had three brothers and two sisters. As each boy reached the age of about ten years, he was sent off to school. Salva's older brothers, Ariik and Ring, had gone to school before him; last year, it had been Salva's turn. His two sisters, Akit and Agnath, did not go to school. Like the other girls in the village, they stayed home and learned from their mother how to keep house.

Most of the time, Salva was glad to be able to go to school. But some days he wished he were still back at home herding cattle.

He and his brothers, along with the sons of his father's other wives, would walk with the herds to the water holes, where there was good grazing. Their responsibilities depended on how old they were. Salva's younger brother, Kuol, was taking care of just one cow; like his brothers before him, he would be in charge of more cows every year. Before Salva had begun going to school, he had helped look after the entire herd, and his younger brother as well.

The boys had to keep an eye on the cows, but the cows did not really need much care. That left plenty of time to play.

Salva and the other boys made cows out of clay. The more cows you made, the richer you were. But they had to be fine, healthy animals. It took time to make a lump of clay look like a good cow. The boys would challenge each other to see who could make the most and best cows.

Other times they would practice with their bows and arrows, shooting at small animals or birds. They weren't very good at this yet, but once in a while they got lucky.

Those were the best days. When one of them managed to kill a ground squirrel or a rabbit, a guinea hen or a grouse, the boys' aimless play halted and there was suddenly a lot of work to do.

Some of them gathered wood to build a fire. Others helped clean and dress the animal. Then they roasted it on the fire.

None of this took place quietly. Salva had his own opinion of how the fire should be built and how long the meat needed to cook, and so did each of the others.

"The fire needs to be bigger."

"It won't last long enough—we need more wood."

"No, it's big enough already."

"Quick, turn it over before it's ruined!"

The juices dripped and sizzled. A delicious smell filled the air.

Finally, they couldn't wait one second longer. There was only enough for each boy to have a few bites, but, oh, how delicious those bites were!

Salva swallowed and turned his eyes back toward the teacher. He wished he hadn't recalled those times, because the memories made him hungry. . . . Milk. When he got home, he would have a bowl of fresh milk, which would keep his belly full until suppertime.

He knew just how it would be. His mother would rise from her work grinding meal and walk around to the side of the house that faced the road. She would shade her eyes with one hand, searching for him. From far off he would see her bright orange headscarf, and he would raise his arm in greeting. By the time he reached the house, she would have gone inside to get his bowl of milk ready for him.

CRACK!

The noise had come from outside. Was it a gunshot? Or just a car backfiring?

The teacher stopped talking for a moment. Every head in the room turned toward the window.

Nothing. Silence.

The teacher cleared his throat, which drew the boys' attention to the front of the room again. He continued the lesson from where he had left off. Then—

CRACK! POP–POP–CRACK!

ACK-ACK-ACK-ACK-ACK-ACK!

Gunfire!

"Everyone, *DOWN!*" the teacher shouted.

Some of the boys moved at once, ducking their heads

and hunching over. Others sat frozen, their eyes and mouths open wide. Salva covered his head with his hands and looked from side to side in panic.

The teacher edged his way along the wall to the window. He took a quick peek outside. The gunfire had stopped, but now people were shouting and running.

"Go quickly, all of you," the teacher said, his voice low and urgent. "Into the bush. Do you hear me? Not home. Don't run home. They will be going into the villages. Stay away from the villages—run into the bush."

He went to the door and looked out again.

"Go! All of you, now!"

The war had started two years earlier. Salva did not understand much about it, but he knew that rebels from the southern part of Sudan, where he and his family lived, were fighting against the government, which was based in the north. Most of the people who lived in the north were Muslim, and the government wanted all of Sudan to become a Muslim country—a place where the beliefs of Islam were followed.

But the people in the south were of different religions and did not want to be forced to practice Islam. They began fighting for independence from the north. The fighting was scattered all around southern Sudan, and now the war had come to where Salva lived.

The boys scrambled to their feet. Some of them were crying. The teacher began hurrying the students out the door.

Salva was near the end of the line. He felt his heart beating so hard that its pulse pounded in his throat and ears. He wanted to shout, "I need to go home! I must go home!" But the words were blocked by the wild thumping in his throat.

When he got to the door, he looked out. Everyone was running—men, children, women carrying babies. The air was full of dust that had been kicked up by all those running feet. Some of the men were shouting and waving guns.

Salva saw all this with one glance.

Then he was running, too. Running as hard as he could, into the bush.

Away from home.

CHAPTER TWO

Southern Sudan, 2008

Nya put the container down and sat on the ground. She always tried not to step on the spiky plants that grew along the path, but their thorns littered the ground everywhere.

She looked at the bottom of her foot. There it was, a big thorn that had broken off right in the middle of her heel. Nya pushed at the skin around the thorn. Then she picked up another thorn and used it to poke and prod at the first one. She pressed her lips together against the pain.

Southern Sudan, 1985

BOOM!

Salva turned and looked. Behind him, a huge black cloud of smoke rose. Flames darted out of its base. Overhead, a jet plane veered away like a sleek evil bird.

In the smoke and dust, he couldn't see the school

building anymore. He tripped and almost fell. No more looking back; it slowed him down.

Salva lowered his head and ran.

He ran until he could not run anymore. Then he walked. For hours, until the sun was nearly gone from the sky.

Other people were walking, too. There were so many of them that they couldn't all be from the school village; they must have come from the whole area.

As Salva walked, the same thoughts kept going through his head in rhythm with his steps. *Where are we going? Where is my family? When will I see them again?*

The people stopped walking when it grew too dark to see the path. At first, everyone stood around uncertainly, speaking in tense whispers or silent with fear.

Then some of the men gathered and talked for a few moments. One of them called out, "Villages—group yourselves by villages. You will find someone you know."

Salva wandered around until he heard the words "Loun-Ariik! The village of Loun-Ariik, here!"

Relief flooded through him. That was his village! He hurried toward the sound of the voice.

A dozen or so people stood in a loose group at the side

of the road. Salva scanned their faces. There was no one from his family. He recognized a few people—a woman with a baby, two men, a teenage girl—but no one he knew well. Still, it was comforting to see them.

They spent the night right there by the road, the men taking shifts to keep watch. The next morning, they began walking again. Salva stayed in the midst of the crowd with the other villagers from Loun-Ariik.

In the early afternoon, he saw a large group of soldiers up ahead.

Word passed through the crowd: "It's the rebels." The rebels—those who were fighting against the government.

Salva passed several rebel soldiers waiting by the side of the road. Each of them held a big gun. Their guns were not pointed at the crowd, but even so, the soldiers seemed fierce and watchful. Some of the rebels then joined the back of the line; now the villagers were surrounded.

What are they going to do to us? Where is my family?

Late in the day, the villagers arrived at the rebel camp. The soldiers ordered them to separate into two groups—men in one group, women and children and the elderly in the other. Teenage boys, it seemed, were considered men, for boys who looked to be only a few years older than Salva were joining the men's group.

Salva hesitated for a moment. He was only eleven, but he was the son of an important family. He was Salva Mawien Dut Ariik, from the village named for his grandfather. His father always told him to act like a man—to follow the example of his older brothers and, in turn, set a good example for Kuol.

Salva took a few steps toward the men.

"Hey!"

A soldier approached Salva and raised his gun.

Salva froze. All he could see was the gun's huge barrel, black and gleaming, as it moved toward his face.

The end of the barrel touched his chin.

Salva felt his knees turn to water. He closed his eyes.

If I die now, I will never see my family again.

Somehow, this thought strengthened him enough to keep him from collapsing in terror.

He took a deep breath and opened his eyes.

The soldier was holding the gun with only one hand. He was not *aiming* it; he was using it to lift Salva's chin so he could get a better look at his face.

"Over there," the soldier said. He moved the gun and pointed it toward the group of women and children.

"You are not a man yet. Don't be in such a hurry!" He laughed and clapped Salva on the shoulder.

Salva scurried over to the women's side.

The next morning, the rebels moved on from the camp. The village men were forced to carry supplies: guns and mortars, shells, radio equipment. Salva watched as one man protested that he did not want to go with the rebels. A soldier hit him in the face with the butt of a gun. The man fell to the ground, bleeding.

After that, no one objected. The men shouldered the heavy equipment and left the camp.

Everyone else began walking again. They went in the opposite direction from the rebels, for wherever the rebels went, there was sure to be fighting.

Salva stayed with the group from Loun-Ariik. It was smaller now, without the men. And except for the infant, Salva was the only child.

That evening they found a barn in which to spend the night. Salva tossed restlessly in the itchy hay.

Where are we going? Where is my family? When will I see them again?

It took him a long time to fall asleep.

*   *   *

Even before he was fully awake, Salva could feel that something was wrong. He lay very still with his eyes closed, trying to sense what it might be.

Finally, he sat up and opened his eyes.

No one else was in the barn.

Salva stood so quickly that for a moment he felt dizzy. He rushed to the door and looked out.

Nobody. Nothing.

They had left him.

He was alone.

CHAPTER THREE

Southern Sudan, 2008

The smudge on the horizon gained color as Nya drew nearer, changing from hazy gray to olive green. The dirt under her feet turned to mud, then sludge, until at last she was ankle-deep in water.

There was always so much life around the pond: other people, mostly women and girls, who had come to fill their own containers; many kinds of birds, all flap and twitter and caw; herds of cattle that had been brought to the good grazing by the young boys who looked after them.

Nya took the hollowed gourd that was tied to the handle of the plastic container. She untied it, scooped up the brown muddy water, and drank. It took two gourdfuls before she felt a little cooler inside.

Nya filled the container all the way to the top. Then she tied the gourd back in place and took the padded cloth doughnut from her pocket. The doughnut went on her head first, followed by the heavy container of water, which she would hold in place with one hand.

With the water balanced on her head, and her foot still

sore from the thorn, Nya knew that going home would take longer than coming had. But she might reach home by noon, if all went well.

The tears were hot in Salva's eyes. Where had everyone gone? Why had they left without waking him?

He knew the answer: because he was a child . . . who might tire easily and slow them down, and complain about being hungry, and cause trouble somehow.

I would not have been any trouble—I would not have complained! . . . What will I do now?

Salva took a few steps to see what he could see. On the far horizon, the sky was hazy from the smoke of the bombs. About a hundred paces in front of him, he could see a small pond. Between the pond and the barn was a house—and, yes, a woman sitting in the sun.

Holding his breath, he crept closer, until he could see her face clearly. The ritual scar patterns on her forehead were familiar: They were Dinka patterns, which meant that she was from the same tribe as Salva.

Salva let out his breath in relief. He was glad that she was not Nuer. The Nuer and the Dinka had a long history of trouble. No one, it seemed, was sure where Nuer land ended and Dinka land began, so each tribe tried to lay claim to the areas richest in water. Over the years, there had been many battles, large and small, between Dinka and Nuer; many people on both sides had been killed. This was not the same as the war that was going on now, between the rebels and the government. The Dinka and the Nuer had been fighting each other for hundreds of years.

The woman looked up and saw him. Salva flinched at her glance. Would she be friendly to a stranger? Would she be angry with him for spending the night in her barn?

But at least he was not alone now, and that knowledge was stronger than the uncertainty about what the woman might do or say to him. He walked toward her. "Good morning, Auntie," he said, his voice trembling.

She nodded at him. She was old, much older than Salva's mother.

He kept quiet, waiting for her to speak.

"You must be hungry," she said at last. She stood and went into the house. A few moments later, she came back out and gave him two handfuls of raw peanuts. Then she sat down again.

"Thank you, Auntie." Squatting on his haunches next to her, Salva shelled the nuts and ate them. He chewed every nut into a paste before he swallowed, trying to make each one last as long as he could.

The woman sat without speaking until he was finished. Then she asked, "Where are your people?"

Salva opened his mouth to speak, but his eyes filled with tears again and he could not answer.

She frowned. "Are you an orphan?"

He shook his head quickly. For a moment, he felt almost angry. He was not an orphan! He had a father and a mother—he had a family!

"I was at school. I ran away from the fighting. I do not know where my family is."

She nodded. "A bad thing, this war. What are you going to do—how will you find them?"

Salva had no answer. He had hoped that the woman might have some answers for him; after all, she was an adult. Instead, she had only questions.

Everything was upside down.

Salva stayed in the woman's barn again that night. He began to make a plan. *Maybe I can stay here until the fighting stops. Then I will go back to my village and find my family.*

He worked hard so she would not send him away. For three days, he fetched firewood from the bush and water from the pond. But the pond was drying up; each day it was harder to fill the gourds.

During the daytime, Salva could hear the distant booming of artillery from the fighting a few miles away. With every shell that exploded he would think of his family, hoping they were safe, wondering desperately when he would be with them again.

On the fourth day, the old woman told him that she was leaving.

"You have seen that the pond is only a puddle now. Winter is coming, and the dry season. And this fighting." She nodded her head in the direction of the noise. "I will go to a different village near water. You cannot stay with me any longer."

Salva stared at her as panic rose inside him. *Why can't I go with her?*

The woman spoke again before he could ask aloud. "The soldiers will leave me alone, an old woman on her own. It would be more dangerous for me to travel with you."

She shook her head in sympathy. "I am sorry I cannot help you anymore," she said. "Wherever it is you walk, just be sure to walk away from the fighting."

Salva stumbled back to the barn. *What will I do, where will I go?* The words repeated themselves a thousand times in his head. It was so strange—he had known the old woman for only a few days, but now he could not imagine what he would do once she was gone.

He sat inside the barn and stared out, looking at nothing. As the light grew dimmer, the noises of evening began—the buzz of insects, the rustling of dry leaves, and another sound . . . voices?

Salva turned his head toward the sound. Yes, it was voices. Some people were walking toward the house—a small group, fewer than a dozen. As they approached, Salva took a sharp breath.

In the fading light he could see the faces of those nearest him. Two of the men had patterns of V-shaped scars on their foreheads. Dinka patterns again—the kind that were given to the boys in Salva's village as part of the ritual of becoming a man.

These people were Dinka, too! Could his family be among them?

CHAPTER FOUR

Southern Sudan, 2008

Nya's mother took the plastic container from her and emptied the water into three large jars. She handed Nya a bowl of boiled sorghum meal and poured a little milk over it.

Nya sat outside in the shade of the house and ate.

When she was done, she took the bowl back inside. Her mother was nursing the baby, Nya's little brother. "Take Akeer with you," her mother said, nodding toward Nya's sister.

Glancing at her younger sister, Nya did not say what she was thinking: that Akeer, who was only five years old, was too small and walked too slowly.

"She needs to learn," her mother said.

Nya nodded. She picked up the plastic container and took Akeer by the hand.

Home for just long enough to eat, Nya would now make her second trip to the pond. To the pond and back—to the pond and back—nearly a full day of walking altogether. This was Nya's daily routine seven months of the year.

Daily. Every single day.

Salva held his breath as he scanned the faces, one by one. Then the air left his lungs and seemed to take all hope with it.

Strangers. No one from his family.

The old woman came up behind him and greeted the group. "Where are you going?" she asked.

A few of the people exchanged uneasy glances. There was no reply.

The woman put her hand on Salva's shoulder. "This one is alone. Will you take him with you?"

Salva saw doubt on the people's faces. Several men at the front of the group began speaking to each other.

"He is a child. He will slow us down."

"Another mouth to feed? It is already hard enough to find food."

"He is too young to do any real work—he'll be of no help to us."

Salva hung his head. They would leave him behind again, just as the others had. . . .

Then a woman in the group reached out and touched

the arm of one of the men. She said nothing but looked first at the man and then at Salva.

The man nodded and turned to the group. "We will take him with us," he said.

Salva looked up quickly. A few in the group were shaking their heads and grumbling.

The man shrugged. "He is Dinka," he said, and began walking again.

The old woman gave Salva a bag of peanuts and a gourd for drinking water. He thanked her and said goodbye. Then he caught up with the group, determined not to lag behind, not to complain, not to be any trouble to anyone. He did not even ask where they were going, for fear that his questions would be unwelcome.

He knew only that they were Dinka and that they were trying to stay away from the war. He had to be content with that.

The days became a never-ending walk. Salva's feet kept time with the thoughts in his head, the same words over and over: *Where is my family? Where is my family?*

Every day he woke and walked with the group, rested at midday, and walked again until dark. They slept on the ground. The terrain changed from scrub to woodland;

they walked among stands of stunted trees. There was little to eat: a few fruits here and there, always either unripe or worm-rotten. Salva's peanuts were gone by the end of the third day.

After about a week, they were joined by more people—another group of Dinka and several members of a tribe called the Jur-chol. Men and women, boys and girls, old and young, walking, walking. . . .

Walking to nowhere.

Salva had never been so hungry. He stumbled along, somehow moving one foot ahead of the other, not noticing the ground he walked on or the forest around him or the light in the sky. Nothing was real except his hunger, once a hollow in his stomach but now a deep buzzing pain in every part of him.

Usually he walked among the Dinka, but today, shuffling along in a daze, he found he had fallen a little behind. Walking next to him was a young man from the Jur-chol. Salva didn't know much about him, except that his name was Buksa.

As they walked along, Buksa slowed down. Salva wondered sluggishly if they shouldn't try to keep up a bit better.

Just then Buksa stopped walking. Salva stopped, too.

But he was too weak and hungry to ask why they were standing still.

Buksa cocked his head and furrowed his brow, listening. They stood motionless for several moments. Salva could hear the noise of the rest of the group ahead of them, a few faint voices, birds calling somewhere in the trees. . . .

He strained his ears. What was it? Jet planes? Bombs? Was the gunfire getting closer, instead of farther away? Salva's fear began to grow until it was even stronger than his hunger. Then—

"Ah." A slow smile spread over Buksa's face. "There. You hear?"

Salva frowned and shook his head.

"Yes, there it is again. Come!" Buksa began walking very quickly. Salva struggled to keep up. Twice Buksa paused to listen, then kept going even faster.

"What—" Salva started to ask.

Buksa stopped abruptly in front of a very large tree. "Yes!" he said. "Now go call the others!"

By now Salva had caught the feeling of excitement. "But what shall I tell them?"

"The bird. The one I was listening to. He led me right here." Buksa's smile was even bigger now. "You see that?"

He pointed up at the branches of the tree. "Beehive. A fine, large one."

Salva hurried off to call the rest of the group. He had heard of this, that the Jur-chol could follow the call of the bird called the honey guide! But he had never seen it done before.

Honey! This night, they would feast!

CHAPTER FIVE

Southern Sudan, 2008

There was a big lake three days' walk from Nya's village. Every year when the rains stopped and the pond near the village dried up, Nya's family moved from their home to a camp near the big lake.

Nya's family did not live by the lake all year round because of the fighting. Her tribe, the Nuer, often fought with the rival Dinka tribe over the land surrounding the lake. Men and boys were hurt and even killed when the two groups clashed. So Nya and the rest of her village lived at the lake only during the five months of the dry season, when both tribes were so busy struggling for survival that the fighting occurred far less often.

Like the pond back home, the lake was dried up. But because it was much bigger than the pond, the clay of the lakebed still held water.

Nya's job at the lake camp was the same as at home: to fetch water. With her hands, she would dig a hole in the damp clay of the lakebed. She kept digging, scooping out handfuls of clay until the hole was as deep as her arm was long. The clay got wetter as she dug, until, at last, water began to seep into the bottom of the hole.

The water that filled the hole was filthy, more mud than liquid. It seeped in so slowly that it took a long time to collect even a few gourdsful. Nya would crouch by the hole, waiting.

Waiting for water. Here, for hours at a time. And every day for five long months, until the rains came and she and her family could return home.

Southern Sudan, 1985

Salva's eye was swollen shut. Buksa's forearms were lumpy and raw. A friend of Buksa's had a fat lip. They all looked as though they had been in a terrible fistfight.

But their injuries weren't bruises. They were bee stings.

A fire had been started under the tree, to smoke the bees out of the hive and make them sleepy. But as Buksa and the other Jur-chol men were removing the hive from the tree, the bees woke up and were not at all happy to discover that their home was being taken away. They expressed their unhappiness very clearly by buzzing, swarming, and stinging. Stinging a lot.

It *was worth it*, Salva thought as he touched his eye gingerly. His belly was a rounded lump stuffed full of honey and beeswax. Nothing had ever tasted so good as those pieces of honeycomb dripping with rich, luscious gold sweetness. Along with everyone else in the group, he had eaten as much as he could hold—and then a little more.

All around him, people were licking their fingers in great satisfaction—except for one Dinka man who had been stung on his *tongue*. It was swollen so badly that he could not close his mouth; he could hardly swallow.

Salva felt very sorry for him. The poor man couldn't even enjoy the honey.

The walking seemed easier now that Salva had something in his belly. He had managed to save one last piece of honeycomb and had wrapped it carefully in a leaf. By the end of the next day, all the honey was gone, but Salva kept the beeswax in his mouth and chewed it for the memory of sweetness.

The group got a little bigger with each passing day. More people joined them—people who had been walking alone or in little clusters of two or three. Salva made it a habit to survey the whole group every morning and evening, searching for his family. But they were never among the newcomers.

One evening a few weeks after Salva had joined the group, he made his usual walk around the fireside, scanning every face in the hope of seeing a familiar one.

Then—

"*Ouch!*"

Salva almost lost his footing as the ground underneath him seemed to move.

A boy jumped to his feet and stood in front of him.

"Hey! That was my hand you stepped on!" The boy spoke Dinka but with a different accent, which meant that he was not from the area around Salva's village.

Salva took a step back. "Sorry. Are you hurt?"

The boy opened and closed his hand a few times, then shrugged. "It's all right. But you really should watch where you're going."

"Sorry," Salva repeated. After a moment's silence, he turned away and began searching the crowd again.

The boy was still looking at him. "Your family?" he asked.

Salva shook his head.

"Me, too," the boy said. He sighed, and Salva heard that sigh all the way to his heart.

Their eyes met. "I'm Salva."

"I'm Marial."

It was good to make a friend.

Marial was the same age as Salva. They were almost the same height. When they walked side by side, their strides were exactly the same length. And the next morning, they began walking together.

"Do you know where we're going?" Salva asked.

Marial tilted his head up and put his hand on his brow to shade his eyes from the rising sun. "East," he said wisely. "We are walking into the morning sun."

Salva rolled his eyes. "I *know* we're going east," he said. "Anyone could tell that. But *where* in the east?"

Marial thought for a moment. "Ethiopia," he said. "East of Sudan is Ethiopia."

Salva stopped walking. "Ethiopia? That is another country! We can't walk all the way there."

"We are walking east," Marial said firmly. "Ethiopia is east."

I can't go to another country, Salva thought. *If I do, my family will never find me.* . . .

Marial put his arm around Salva's shoulders. He seemed to know what Salva was thinking, for he said, "It doesn't matter. Don't you know that if we keep walking east, we'll go all the way around the world and come right back here to Sudan? That's when we'll find our families!"

Salva had to laugh. They were both laughing as they started walking again, arm in arm, their strides matching perfectly.

More than a month had passed since Salva had run from his school into the bush. The group was now walking in the land of the Atuot people.

In the Dinka language, the Atuot were called "the people of the lion." Their region was inhabited by large herds of antelope, wildebeest, gnus—and the lions that preyed on them. The Dinka told stories about the Atuot. When an Atuot person died, he came back to Earth as a lion, with a great hunger for the human flesh he once had. The lions in the Atuot region were said to be the fiercest in the world.

Nights became uneasy. Salva woke often to the sound of roars in the distance and sometimes to the death-squeal of an animal under a lion's claws.

One morning he woke bleary-eyed after a poor sleep. He rubbed his eyes, rose, and stumbled after Marial as they began walking yet again.

"Salva?"

It was not Marial who had spoken. The voice had come from behind them.

Salva turned. His mouth fell open in amazement, but he could not speak.

"*Salva!*"

CHAPTER SIX

Southern Sudan, 2008

Nya's family had been coming to the lake camp for generations; Nya herself had been there every year since she was born. One thing she liked about the camp was that, even though she had to dig in the clay and wait for water, she did not have to make the two long trips to the pond every day. But this year she realized for the first time that her mother hated the camp.

They had no house and had to sleep in makeshift shelters. They could not bring most of their things, so they had to make do with whatever was at hand. And for much of each day, they had to dig for water.

But the worst was the look on her mother's face when Nya's father and older brother, Dep, went off to hunt.

Fear.

Her mother was afraid. Afraid that the men in the family would run into Dinka tribesmen somewhere, that they would fight and get injured—or worse.

They had been lucky all these years. No one from Nya's

family had been hurt or killed by Dinka. But she knew other families in the village who had lost loved ones in this way.

Nya could see the questions in her mother's face every morning: Would they be lucky again?

Or was it now their turn to lose someone?

Southern Sudan, 1985

Salva's mouth closed and opened again, as if he were a fish. He tried to speak, but no sound came out of his throat. He tried to move, but his feet seemed stuck to the ground.

"Salva!" the man said again, and hurried toward him. When the man was only a few steps away, Salva suddenly found his voice.

"Uncle!" he cried out, and ran into the man's arms.

Uncle Jewiir was the younger brother of Salva's father. Salva hadn't seen him in at least two years, because Uncle had been in the army.

Uncle must know about the war and the fighting! Maybe he will know where my family is!

But these hopes were dashed as soon as Uncle spoke. "Are you alone? Where is your family?" he asked.

Salva hardly knew where to begin his answer. It seemed like years since he had run away from his school and into the bush. But he told his uncle everything as best he could.

As Salva spoke, Uncle nodded or shook his head. His face became very solemn when Salva told him that he had not seen nor heard a single word of his family in all that time. Salva's voice trailed off, and he lowered his head. He was glad to see Uncle again, but it looked as if he might not be much help either.

Uncle was quiet for a moment. Then he patted Salva's shoulder. "Eh, Nephew!" he said in a cheerful voice. "We are together now, so I will look after you!"

It turned out that Uncle had joined the group three days earlier, but since there were more than thirty people traveling together, they had not found each other until now. As they began walking, Salva saw that Uncle had a gun—a rifle that he carried on a strap over one shoulder. Already Salva could tell that because of his army experience and because he had a gun, Uncle was seen by the group as a kind of leader.

"Yes, when I left the army they let me keep my rifle," Uncle said. "So I am going to shoot us a fine meal as soon as we come across anything worth eating!"

Uncle was true to his word. That very day he shot a young antelope, the kind called a topi. Salva could hardly wait for it to be skinned and butchered and roasted. As the smoky, meaty aroma filled the air, he had to keep swallowing the saliva that flooded his mouth.

Uncle laughed as he watched Salva gobble down his first piece of the meat. "Salva, you have teeth! You are supposed to use them when you eat!"

Salva could not reply; he was too busy stuffing another chunk of the delicious charred meat into his mouth.

Even though the topi was a small one, there was more than enough meat for everyone in the group. But it did not take long for Salva to regret his haste in eating. After so many weeks of near starvation, his stomach rebelled mightily: He spent most of the night vomiting.

Salva was not alone. Whenever his heaving stomach woke him, he would hurry to the edge of the camp to vomit and find others there doing the same. At one point, Salva found himself in a line of half a dozen people, all in an identical pose—bent over, holding their stomachs, and waiting for the next wave of nausea.

It might have been funny if he hadn't felt so miserable.

*   *   *

The group continued to walk through the land of the At-uot. Every day they saw lions, usually resting in the shade of small trees. Once, in the distance, they saw a lion chasing a topi. The topi escaped, but along the path Salva saw the bones of prey that had not been so fortunate.

Salva and Marial still walked together, staying close to Uncle. Sometimes Uncle would walk with the other men and talk seriously about the journey. At those times, Salva and Marial would drop back respectfully, but Salva always tried to keep Uncle in sight. And he slept near Uncle at night.

One day the group began walking in the late afternoon, with hopes of reaching a water hole before settling down for the night. But there was no water anywhere, though they searched for miles. They kept walking, into the night and through the night. For ten hours they walked, and by dawn everyone was exhausted.

Uncle and the other leaders finally decided that the group had to rest. Salva took two steps off the path and fell asleep almost before he lay down.

He did not wake until he felt Uncle's hand shaking his shoulder. As he opened his eyes, he heard wailing. Someone was crying. Salva blinked away the sleepiness and looked at Uncle, whose face was very solemn.

"I am sorry, Salva," Uncle said quietly. "Your friend . . ."

Marial? Salva looked around. He *should be somewhere nearby. . . . I don't remember if he slept near me—I was so tired—perhaps he has gone to find something to eat—*

Uncle stroked Salva's head as if he were a baby. "I am sorry," he said again.

A cold fist seemed to grip Salva's heart.

CHAPTER SEVEN

Southern Sudan, 2008

Nya sat on the floor. She reached out and took her little sister's hand.

Akeer did not seem to notice. She lay curled on her side, hardly moving, silent except for an occasional whimper.

Her silence frightened Nya. Only two days earlier, Akeer had complained noisily and at length about the pains in her stomach. Nya had been annoyed by all the whining. Now she felt guilty, for she could see that her sister no longer had enough strength to complain.

Nya knew many people who suffered from the same illness. First cramps and stomachache, then diarrhea. Sometimes fever, too. Most of the adults and older children who fell ill recovered at least enough to work again, although they might continue to suffer off and on for years.

For the elderly and for small children, the illness could be dangerous. Unable to hold anything in their systems, many of them starved to death, even with food right in front of them.

Nya's uncle, the chief of their village, knew of a medical clinic a few days' walk away. He told Nya's family that if they could take Akeer there, doctors would give her medicine to help her get better.

But a trip like that would be very difficult for Akeer. Should they stay at the camp and let her rest so she might heal on her own? Or should they begin the long hard walk— and hope they reached help in time?

Southern Sudan, 1985

ॐ

The walking began again. Salva shook with terror inside and out.

He clung to Uncle like a baby or a little boy, hanging on to his hand or shirttail when he could, never letting Uncle get farther than an arm's length away. He looked around constantly: Every movement in the grass was a lion stalking, every stillness a lion waiting to spring.

Marial was gone—vanished into the night. He would never have wandered away from the group on his own. His disappearance could mean only one thing.

Lion.

A lion had been hungry enough to approach the group as they slept. A few men had been keeping watch, but in the dark of night, with the wind rippling through the long grass, the lion could easily have crept close without being seen. It had sought out prey that was small and motionless: Marial, sleeping.

And it had taken him away, leaving only a few splotches of blood near the path.

If it hadn't been for Uncle, Salva might have gone crazy with fear. Uncle spoke to him all morning in a steady, low voice.

"Salva, I have a gun. I will shoot any lion that comes near."

"Salva, I will stay awake tonight and keep watch."

"Salva, we will soon be out of lion country. Everything will be all right."

Listening to Uncle, hurrying to stay close to him, Salva was able to make his feet move despite the cold terror throughout his whole body.

But nothing was all right. He had lost his family, and now he had lost his friend as well.

No one had heard any screaming in the night. Salva hoped with all his heart that the lion had killed Marial instantly—that his friend hadn't had time to feel fear or pain.

*　　*　　*

The landscape grew greener. The air smelled of water.

"The Nile," Uncle said. "We will soon come to the Nile River and cross to the other side."

The Nile: the longest river in the world, the mother of all life in Sudan. Uncle explained that they would come to the river at one of its broadest stretches.

"It will not even look like a river. It will look like a big lake. We will spend a long time crossing to the other side."

"And what is on the other side?" Salva whispered, still fearful.

"Desert," Uncle answered. "And after that, Ethiopia."

Salva's eyes filled with tears. Marial had been right about Ethiopia. *How I wish he were here, so I could tell him I was wrong.*

Salva stood on the bank of the Nile. Here, as Uncle had said, the river formed a big lake.

The group would cross the Nile in boats, Uncle said. It would take a whole day to reach the islands in the middle of the lake, and another day to get to the far shore.

Salva frowned. He saw no boats anywhere.

Uncle smiled at Salva's puzzled expression. "What, you didn't bring your own boat?" he said. "Then I hope you are a good swimmer!"

Salva lowered his head. He knew that Uncle was teasing, but he felt so tired—tired of worrying about his family, tired of thinking about poor Marial, tired of walking and not knowing where they were going. The least Uncle could do was tell him the truth about the boats.

Uncle put his arm around Salva's shoulders. "You'll see. We have a lot of work to do."

Salva staggered forward with yet another enormous load of reeds in his arms. Everyone was busy. Some people were cutting down the tall papyrus grass by the water's edge. Others, like Salva, gathered up the cut stalks and took them to the boatbuilders.

Among the group were a few people whose home villages had been near rivers or lakes. They knew how to tie the reeds together and weave them cleverly to form shallow canoes.

Everyone worked quickly, although there was no way of knowing whether they had to hurry or not, no way of knowing how near the war was. The fighting could be miles away—or a plane carrying bombs could fly overhead at any moment.

It was hard work running back and forth between those cutting and those weaving. But Salva found that the work was helping him feel a little better. He was too busy to worry much. Doing something, even carrying big, awkward piles of slippery reeds, was better than doing nothing.

Every time Salva delivered a load of reeds, he would pause for a few moments to admire the skills of the boat-builders. The long reeds were laid out in neat bunches. Each end of a bunch would be tied together tightly. Then the bunch of reeds was pulled apart in the middle to form a hollow, and the two sides were tied all along their length to make a basic boat shape. More layers of reeds were added and tied to make the bottom of the boat. Salva watched, fascinated, as little by little the curve of a prow and low sides grew from the piles of reeds.

It took two full days for the group to build enough canoes. Each canoe was tested; a few did not float well and had to be fixed. Then more reeds were tied together to form paddles.

At last, everything was ready. Salva got into a canoe between Uncle and another man. He gripped the sides of the boat tightly as it floated out onto the Nile.

CHAPTER EIGHT

Southern Sudan, 2008

It was like music, the sound of Akeer's laugh.

Nya's father had decided that Akeer needed a doctor. So Nya and her mother had taken Akeer to the special place—a big white tent full of people who were sick or hurt, with doctors and nurses to help them. After just two doses of medicine, Akeer was nearly her old self again—still thin and weak but able to laugh as Nya sat on the floor next to her cot and played a clapping game with her.

The nurse, a white woman, was talking to Nya's mother.

"Her sickness came from the water," the nurse explained. "She should drink only good clean water. If the water is dirty, you should boil it for a count of two hundred before she drinks it."

Nya's mother nodded that she understood, but Nya could see the worry in her eyes.

The water from the holes in the lakebed could be collected only in tiny amounts. If her mother tried to boil such a small amount, the pot would be dry long before they could count to two hundred.

It was a good thing, then, that they would soon be returning to the village. The water that Nya fetched from the pond in the plastic jug could be boiled before they drank it.

But what about next year at camp? And the year after that?

And even at home, whenever Nya made the long hot walk to the pond, she had to drink as soon as she got there.

She would never be able to stop Akeer from doing the same.

Southern Sudan, 1985

The lake's surface was calm, and once the boats had pulled away from the shore, there was not much to see—just water and more water.

They paddled for hours. The scenery and motion were so monotonous that Salva might have slept, except he was afraid that if he did, he might fall over the side. He kept himself awake by counting the strokes of Uncle's paddle and trying to gauge how far the canoe traveled with every twenty strokes.

Finally, the boats pulled up to an island in the middle of the river. This was where the fishermen of the Nile lived and worked.

Salva was amazed by what he saw in the fishing community. It was the first place in their weeks of walking that had an abundance of food. The villagers ate a lot of fish, of course, and hippo and crocodile meat as well. But even more impressive were the number of crops they grew: cassava, sugar cane, yams. . . . It was easy to grow food when there was a whole river to water the crops!

None of the travelers had money or anything of value to trade, so they had to beg for food. The exception was Uncle: The fishermen gave him food without having to be asked. Salva could not tell if this was because Uncle seemed to be the leader of the group or because they were afraid of his gun.

Uncle shared his food with Salva—a piece of sugar cane to suck on right away, then fish that they cooked over a fire and yams roasted in the ashes.

The sugar-cane juice soothed the sharpest edge of Salva's hunger. He was able to eat the rest of the meal slowly, making each bite last a long time.

At home, Salva had never been hungry. His family owned many cattle; they were among the better-off families in their village of Loun-Ariik. They ate mostly porridge made from sorghum and milk. Every so often, his father went to the marketplace by bicycle and brought home bags of beans and rice. These had been grown elsewhere, because few crops could be raised in the dry semi-desert region of Loun-Ariik.

As a special treat, his father sometimes bought mangoes. A bag of mangoes was awkward to carry, especially when the bicycle was already loaded with other goods. So he wedged the mangoes into the spokes of his bicycle wheels. When Salva ran to greet him, he could see the green-skinned mangoes spinning gaily in a blur as his father pedaled.

Salva would take a mango from the spokes almost before his father had dismounted. His mother would peel it for him, its juicy insides the same color as her headscarf. She would slice the flesh away from the big flat seed. Salva loved the sweet slices, but his favorite part was the seed. There was always plenty of fruit that clung stubbornly to the seed. He would nibble and suck at it to get every last shred, making it last for hours.

There were no mangoes among the fishermen's great

stores, but sucking on his piece of sugar cane reminded Salva of those happier times. He wondered if he would ever again see his father riding a bicycle with mangoes in its spokes.

As the sun touched the horizon, the fishermen abruptly went into their tents. They weren't really tents—just white mosquito netting hung or draped to make a space so they could lie down inside. Not one fisherman stayed to talk or eat more or do anything else. It was almost as if they all vanished at the same moment.

Only a few minutes later, mosquitoes rose up from the water, from the reeds, from everywhere. Huge dark clouds of them appeared, their high-pitched whine filling the air. Thousands, maybe millions, of hungry mosquitoes massed so thickly that in one breath Salva could have ended up with a mouthful if he wasn't careful. And even if he was, they were everywhere—in his eyes, nose, ears, on every part of his body.

The fishermen stayed in their nets the whole night long. They had even dug channels from inside the nets to just beyond them so they could urinate without having to leave their little tents.

It didn't matter how often Salva swatted at the mosquitoes, or that one swat killed dozens at a time. For every one he killed, it seemed that hundreds more swarmed in to take its place. With their high singing whine constantly in his ears, Salva slapped and waved at them in frustration all night long.

No one in the group got any sleep. The mosquitoes made sure of that.

In the morning, Salva was covered with bites. The worst ones were in the exact middle of his back, where he couldn't reach to scratch. Those he could reach, though, he scratched until they bled.

The travelers got into the boats one more time, to paddle from the island to the other side of the Nile. The fishermen had warned the group to take plenty of water for the next stretch of their journey. Salva still had the gourd that the old woman had given him. Others in the group had gourds too, or plastic bottles. But there were some who did not have a container. They tore strips from their clothing and soaked them in a desperate attempt to carry at least a little water with them.

Ahead lay the most difficult part of their journey: the Akobo desert.

CHAPTER NINE

Southern Sudan, 2008

Nya's family had been back in the village for several months the day the visitors came; in fact, it was nearly time to leave for the camp again. As the jeep drove up, most of the children ran to meet it. Shy about meeting strangers, Nya hung back.

Two men emerged from the jeep. They spoke to the biggest boys, including Nya's brother, Dep, who led them to the home of the village's chief, his and Nya's uncle.

The chief came out of his house to greet the visitors. They sat in the shade of the house with some of the other village men and drank tea together and talked for a while.

"What are they talking about?" Nya asked Dep.

"Something about water," Dep replied.

Water? The nearest water was the pond, of course, half a morning's walk away.

Anyone could have told them that.

Salva had never seen anything like the desert. Around his village, Loun-Ariik, enough grass and shrubs grew to feed the grazing cattle. There were even trees. But here in the desert, nothing green could survive except tiny evergreen acacia bushes, which somehow endured the long winter months with almost no water.

Uncle said it would take three days to cross the Akobo. Salva's shoes stood no chance against the hot stony desert ground. The soles, made from rubber tire treads, had already been reduced to shreds held together with a little leather and a great deal of hope. After only a few minutes, Salva had to kick off the flapping shreds and continue barefoot.

The first day in the desert felt like the longest day Salva had ever lived through. The sun was relentless and eternal: There was neither wisp of cloud nor whiff of breeze for relief. Each minute of walking in that arid heat felt like an hour. Even breathing became an effort: Every breath Salva took seemed to drain strength rather than restore it.

Thorns gored his feet. His lips became cracked and

parched. Uncle cautioned him to make the water in his gourd last as long as possible. It was the hardest thing Salva had ever done, taking only tiny sips when his body cried out for huge gulps of thirst-quenching, life-giving water.

The worst moment of the day happened near the end. Salva stubbed his bare toe on a rock, and his whole toenail came off.

The pain was terrible. Salva tried to bite his lip, but the awfulness of that never-ending day was too much for him. He lowered his head, and the tears began to flow.

Soon he was crying so hard that he could hardly get his breath. He could not think; he could barely see. He had to slow down, and for the first time on the long journey, he began to lag behind the group. Stumbling about blindly, he did not notice the group drawing farther and farther ahead of him.

As if by magic, Uncle was suddenly at his side.

"Salva Mawien Dut Ariik!" he said, using Salva's full name, loud and clear.

Salva lifted his head, the sobs interrupted by surprise.

"Do you see that group of bushes?" Uncle said, pointing. "You need only to walk as far as those bushes. Can you do that, Salva Mawien Dut Ariik?"

Salva wiped his eyes with the back of his hand. He could see the bushes; they did not look too far away.

Uncle reached into his bag. He took out a tamarind and handed it to Salva.

Chewing on the sour juicy fruit made Salva feel a little better.

When they reached the bushes, Uncle pointed out a clump of rocks up ahead and told Salva to walk as far as the rocks. After that, a lone acacia . . . another clump of rocks . . . a spot bare of everything except sand.

Uncle continued in this way for the rest of the walk. Each time, he spoke to Salva using his full name. Each time, Salva would think of his family and his village, and he was somehow able to keep his wounded feet moving forward, one painful step at a time.

At last, the sun was reluctantly forced from the sky. A blessing of darkness fell across the desert, and it was time to rest.

The next day was a precise copy of the one before: the sun and the heat and, worst of all to Salva's mind, a landscape that was utterly unchanged. The same rocks. The same acacias. The same dust. There was not a thing to indicate that the group was making any progress at all across the desert. Salva felt as if he had walked for hours while staying in exactly the same place.

The fierce heat sent up shimmering waves that made everything look wobbly. Or was he the one who was wobbling? That large clump of rocks up ahead—it almost seemed to be moving. . . .

It *was* moving. It was not rocks at all.

It was people.

Salva's group drew nearer. Salva counted nine men, all of them collapsed on the sand.

One made a small, desperate motion with his hand. Another tried to raise his head but fell back again. None of them made a sound.

As Salva watched, he realized that five of the men were completely motionless.

One of the women in Salva's group pushed forward and knelt down. She opened her container of water.

"What are you doing?" a man called. "You cannot save them!"

The woman did not answer. When she looked up, Salva could see tears in her eyes. She shook her head, then poured a little water onto a cloth and began to wet the lips of one of the men on the sand.

Salva looked at the hollow eyes and the cracked lips

of the men lying on the hot sand, and his own mouth felt so dry that he nearly choked when he tried to swallow.

"If you give them your water, you will not have enough for yourself!" the same voice shouted. "It is useless—they will die, and you will die with them!"

CHAPTER TEN

Southern Sudan, 2008

The men finished their meeting. They all stood and walked past Nya's house. Nya joined the crowd of children following them.

A few minutes' walk beyond her house, there was a tree. The men stopped at the tree, and the strangers talked to Nya's uncle some more.

There was another tree some fifty paces past the first one. With Nya's uncle beside him, one of the men stopped at the halfway point. The other man walked the rest of the way and examined the second tree.

The first man called out to his friend in a language Nya did not understand. The friend answered in the same language, but as he walked back toward the group, he translated for the chief, and Nya could hear him.

"This is the spot, halfway between the two largest trees. We will find the water here."

Nya shook her head. What were they talking about? She knew that place like the back of her own hand. It was there, between the two trees, that the village sometimes gathered to sing and talk around a big fire.

There wasn't a single drop of water on that spot, unless it was raining!

Salva reached for his gourd. He knew it to be half full, but suddenly it felt much lighter, as if there was hardly any water left in it.

Uncle Jewiir must have guessed what he was thinking.

"No, Salva," he murmured. "You are too small, and not strong enough yet. Without water you will not survive the rest of the walk. Some of the others—they will be able to manage better than you."

Sure enough, there were now three women giving water to the men on the ground.

Like a miracle, the small amounts of water revived them. They were able to stagger to their feet and join the group as the walking continued.

But their five dead companions were left behind. There were no tools with which to dig, and besides, burying the dead men would have taken too much time.

Salva tried not to look as he walked past the bodies, but his eyes were drawn in their direction. He knew what would happen. Vultures would find the bodies and strip them of their rotting flesh until only the bones remained. He felt sick at the thought of those men—first dying in such a horrible way, and then having even their corpses ravaged.

If he were older and stronger, would he have given water to those men? Or would he, like most of the group, have kept his water for himself?

It was the group's third day in the desert. By sunset, they would be out of the desert, and after that, it would not be far to the Itang refugee camp in Ethiopia.

As they trudged through the heat, Salva finally had a chance to talk to Uncle about a worry that had been growing like a long shadow across his thoughts. "Uncle, if I am in Ethiopia, how will my parents ever find me? When will I be able to go back to Loun-Ariik?"

"I have talked to the others here," Uncle said. "We believe that the village of Loun-Ariik was attacked and probably burned. Your family . . ." Uncle paused and looked away. When he looked back again, his face was solemn.

"Salva, few people survived the attack on the village. Anyone still alive would have fled into the bush, and no one knows where they are now."

Salva was silent for a moment. Then he said, "At least you will be there with me. In Ethiopia."

Uncle's voice was gentle. "No, Salva. I am going to take you to the refugee camp, but then I will return to Sudan, to fight in the war."

Salva stopped walking and clutched at Uncle's arm. "But, Uncle, I will have no one! Who will be my family?"

Uncle gently loosened Salva's grip so he could take the boy's hand in his. "There will be many other people in the camp. You will become friends with some of them— you will make a kind of family there. They, too, will need people they can depend on."

Salva shook his head, unable to imagine what life would be like in the camp without Uncle. He squeezed Uncle's hand tightly.

Uncle stood quietly and said nothing more.

He knows it will be hard for me, Salva realized. *He does not want to leave me there, but he has to go back and fight for our people. I mustn't act like a baby—I must try to be strong. . . .*

Salva swallowed hard. "Uncle, when you go back to Sudan, you might meet my parents somewhere. You could tell them where I am. Or you could talk to those you meet, and ask where the people of Loun-Ariik are now."

Uncle did not answer right away. Then he said, "Of course I will do that, Nephew."

Salva felt a tiny spark of hope. With Uncle looking for his family, there was a chance they might all be together again one day.

No one in the group had eaten anything for two days. Their water was nearly gone. Only the vision of leaving the desert kept them moving through the heat and the dust.

Early that afternoon, they came across the first evidence that the desert was receding: a few stunted trees near a shallow pool of muddy water. The water was unfit to drink, but a dead stork lay by the pond's edge. Immediately, the group began to make preparations to cook and eat the bird. Salva helped gather twigs for the fire.

As the bird roasted, Salva could hardly keep his eyes off it. There would only be enough for a bite or two for each person, but he could hardly wait.

Then he heard loud voices. Along with the rest of the

group, he turned and saw six men coming toward them. As the men approached, he could see that they were armed with guns and machetes.

The men began shouting.

"Sit down!"

"Hands on your heads!"

"All of you! Now!"

Everyone in the group sat down at once. Salva was afraid of the weapons, and he could see that the others were, too.

One of the men walked among the group and stopped in front of Uncle. Salva could tell by the ritual scarring on the man's face that he was from the Nuer tribe.

"Are you with the rebels?" the man asked.

"No," Uncle answered.

"Where have you come from? Where are you going?"

"We come from the west of the Nile," Uncle said. "We are going to Itang, to the refugee camp."

The man told Uncle to get up and leave his gun where it was. Two of the other men took Uncle to a tree several yards away and tied him to it.

Then the men moved among the group. If anyone was carrying a bag, the men opened it and took whatever was in it. They ordered some people to remove their clothing and took that, too.

Salva was trembling. Even in the midst of his fear, he realized that for the first time on the trip, it was a good thing to be the youngest and smallest: The men would not be interested in his clothes.

When the men had finished their looting, they picked up Uncle's gun. Then they walked to the tree where Uncle was tied up.

Maybe they will leave us alone now that they have robbed us, Salva thought.

He heard them laughing.

As Salva watched, one of the men aimed his gun at Uncle.

Three shots rang out. Then the men ran away.

CHAPTER ELEVEN

Southern Sudan, 2008

After the two men left the village, the task of clearing more of the land between the trees began. It was very hard work: The smaller trees and bushes had to be burned or uprooted. The long grass had to be scythed and hoed under. It was dangerous work, too, as poisonous snakes and scorpions hid in the grass.

Nya was still making the two daily trips to the pond. Each time she returned, she could see that slowly but surely the patch of cleared earth was growing larger.

The earth was dry and rock-hard. Nya felt puzzled and doubtful: How could there be water in such a place?

And when she asked Dep that question, he shook his head. She could see the doubt in his eyes, too.

Southern Sudan and Ethiopia, 1985

They buried Uncle in a hole about two feet deep, a hole that had already been made by some kind of animal. Out of respect for him, the group walked no more that day but took time to mourn the man who had been their leader.

Salva was too numb to think, and when thoughts did come to him, they seemed silly. He was annoyed that they would not be able to eat after all: While the men had been looting the group, more birds had arrived and pecked at the roasted stork until it was nothing but bones.

The time for grief was short, and the walking began again soon after dark. Despite the numbness in his heart, Salva was amazed to find himself walking faster and more boldly than he had before.

Marial was gone. Uncle was gone, too, murdered by those Nuer men right before Salva's eyes. Marial and Uncle were no longer by his side, and they never would be again, but Salva knew that both of them would have wanted him to survive, to finish the trip and reach the Itang refugee camp safely. It was almost as if they had left their strength with him, to help him on his journey.

He could not think of any other explanation for the way he felt. But there was no doubt: Beneath his terrible sadness, he felt stronger.

Now that Salva was without Uncle's care and protection, the group's attitude toward him changed. Once again, they grumbled that he was too young and small, that he might slow them down or start crying again, as he had in the desert.

No one shared anything with him, neither food nor company. Uncle had always shared the animals and birds he shot with everyone in the group. But it seemed they had all forgotten that, for Salva now had to beg for scraps, which were given grudgingly.

The way they were treating him made Salva feel stronger still. *There is no one left to help me. They think I am weak and useless.*

Salva lifted his head proudly. *They are wrong, and I will prove it.*

Salva had never before seen so many people in one place at the same time. How could there be this many people in the world?

More than hundreds. More than thousands. Thousands upon thousands.

People in lines and masses and clumps. People milling around, standing, sitting or crouching on the ground, lying down with their legs curled up because there was not enough room to stretch out.

The refugee camp at Itang was filled with people of all ages—men, women, girls, small children. . . . But most of the refugees were boys and young men who had run away from their villages when the war came. They had run because they were in double danger: from the war itself and from the armies on both sides. Young men and sometimes even boys were often forced to join the fighting, which was why their families and communities—including Salva's schoolmaster—had sent the boys running into the bush at the first sign of fighting.

Children who arrived at the refugee camp without their families were grouped together, so Salva was separated at once from the people he had traveled with. Even though they had not been kind to him, at least he had known them. Now, among strangers once again, he felt uncertain and maybe even afraid.

As he walked through the camp with several other boys, Salva glanced at every face he passed. Uncle had said that no one knew where his family was for certain . . . so wasn't there at least a chance that they might be here in the camp?

Salva looked around at the masses of people stretched out as far as he could see. He felt his heart sink a little, but he clenched his hands into fists and made himself a promise.

If they are here, I will find them.

After so many weeks of walking, Salva found it strange to be staying in one place. During that long, terrible trek, finding a safe place to stop and stay for a while had been desperately important. But now that he was at the camp, he felt restless—almost as if he should begin walking again.

The camp was safe from the war. There were no men with guns or machetes, no planes with bombs overhead. On the evening of his very first day, Salva was given a bowl of boiled maize to eat, and another one the next morning. Already things were better here than they had been during the journey.

During the afternoon of the second day, Salva picked his way slowly through the crowds. Eventually, he found himself standing near the gate that was the main entrance to the camp, watching the new arrivals enter. It did not seem as if the camp could possibly hold any more, but still they kept coming: long lines of people, some emaciated, some hurt or sick, all exhausted.

As Salva scanned the faces, a flash of orange caught his eye.

Orange . . . an orange headscarf . . .

He began pushing and stumbling past people. Someone spoke to him angrily, but he did not stop to excuse himself. He could still see the vivid spot of orange—yes, it was a headscarf—the woman's back was to him, but she was tall, like his mother—he had to catch up, there were too many people in the way—

A half-sob broke free from Salva's lips. He mustn't lose track of her!

CHAPTER TWELVE

Southern Sudan, 2009

An iron giraffe.

A red giraffe that made very loud noises.

The giraffe was a tall drill that had been brought to the village by the two men who had visited earlier. They had returned with a crew of ten more men and two trucks—one hauling the giraffe-drill along with other mysterious equipment, and the other loaded with plastic pipe. Meanwhile, the land was still being cleared.

Nya's mother tied the baby on her back and walked with several other women to a place between the village and the pond. They collected piles of rocks and stones and tied them up into bundles using sturdy cloth. They balanced the bundles on their heads, walked back to the drilling site, and emptied the rocks onto the ground.

Other villagers, using tools borrowed from the visitors, pounded the rocks to break them up into gravel. Many loads of gravel would be needed. Nya didn't know why. The piles of gravel grew larger each day.

The clangor of machinery and hammer greeted Nya each time she returned from the pond—unfamiliar noises that mingled with the voices of men shouting and women singing. It was the sound of people working hard together.

But it did not sound at all like water.

"Mother! Mother, please!"

Salva opened his mouth to call out again. But the words did not come. Instead, he closed his mouth, lowered his head, and turned away.

The woman in the orange headscarf was not his mother. He knew this for certain, even though she was still far away and he had not seen her face.

Uncle's words came back to him: *"The village of Loun-Ariik was attacked . . . burned. Few people survived . . . no one knows where they are now."*

In the moment before calling out to the woman a second time, Salva realized what Uncle had truly meant—something Salva had known in his heart for a long time:

His family was gone. They had been killed by bullets or bombs, starvation or sickness—it did not matter how. What mattered was that Salva was on his own now.

He felt as though he were standing on the edge of a giant hole—a hole filled with the black despair of nothingness.

I am alone now.

I am all that is left of my family.

His father, who had sent Salva to school . . . brought him treats, like mangoes . . . trusted him to take care of the herd. . . . His mother, always ready with food and milk and a soft hand to stroke Salva's head. His brothers and sisters, whom he had laughed with and played with and looked after. . . . He would never see them again.

How can I go on without them?

But how can I not go on? They would want me to sur-vive . . . to grow up and make something of my life . . . to honor their memories.

What was it Uncle had said during that first terrible day in the desert? *"Do you see that group of bushes? You need only to walk as far as those bushes. . . ."*

Uncle had helped him get through the desert that way, bit by bit, one step at a time. Perhaps . . . perhaps Salva could get through life at the camp in the same way.

I *need only to get through the rest of this day*, he told himself.

This day and no other.

If someone had told Salva that he would live in the camp for *six years*, he would never have believed it.

Six years later: July 1991

෯ස

"They are going to close the camp. Everyone will have to leave."

"That's impossible. Where will we go?"

"That's what they're saying. Not just this camp. All of them."

The rumors skittered around the camp. Everyone was uneasy. As the days went by, the uneasiness grew into fear.

Salva was almost seventeen years old now—a young man. He tried to learn what he could about the rumors by talking to the aid workers in the camp. They told him that the Ethiopian government was near collapse. The refugee camps were run by foreign aid groups, but it was the government that permitted them to operate. If the government fell, what would the new rulers do about the camps?

When that question was answered, no one was ready. One rainy morning, as Salva walked toward the school tent, long lines of trucks were arriving. Masses of armed soldiers poured out of the trucks and ordered everyone to leave.

The orders were not just to leave the camp but to leave Ethiopia.

Immediately, there was chaos. It was as if the people ceased to be people and instead became an enormous herd of panicked, stampeding two-legged creatures.

Salva was caught up in the surge. His feet barely touched the ground as he was swept along by the crowd of thousands of people running and screaming. The rain, which was falling in torrents, added to the uproar.

The soldiers fired their guns into the air and chased the people away from the camp. But once they were beyond the area surrounding the camp, the soldiers continued to drive them onward, shouting and shooting.

As he dashed ahead, Salva heard snatches of talk.

"The river."

"They're chasing us toward the river!"

Salva knew which river they meant: the Gilo River, which was along the border between Ethiopia and Sudan.

They are driving us back to Sudan, Salva thought. *They will force us to cross the river. . . .*

It was the rainy season. Swollen by the rains, the Gilo's current would be merciless.

The Gilo was well known for something else, too.

Crocodiles.

CHAPTER THIRTEEN

Southern Sudan, 2009

Nya thought it was funny: You had to have water to find water. Water had to be flowing constantly into the borehole to keep the drill running smoothly.

The crew drove to the pond and back several times a day. The pond water was piped into what looked like a giant plastic bag—a bag big enough to fill the entire bed of the truck.

The bag sprang a leak. The leak had to be patched.

The patch sprang a leak. The crew patched the patch.

Then the bag sprang another leak. The drilling could not go on.

The drilling crew was discouraged by the leaks. They wanted to stop working. But their boss kept them going. All the workers wore the same blue coveralls; still, Nya could tell who was the boss. He was one of the two men who had first come to the village. The other man seemed to be his main assistant.

The boss would encourage the workers and laugh and joke with them. If that didn't work, he would talk to them earnestly and try to persuade them. And if *that* didn't work, he would get angry.

He didn't get angry very often. He kept working—and kept the others working, too.

They patched the bag again. The drilling went on.

Ethiopia–Sudan–Kenya, 1991–92

Hundreds of people lined the riverbank. The soldiers were forcing some of them into the water, prodding them with their rifle butts, shooting into the air.

Other people, afraid of the soldiers and their guns, were leaping into the water on their own. They were immediately swept downstream by the powerful current.

As Salva crouched on the bank and watched, a young man near him plunged into the water. The current carried him swiftly downstream, but he was also making a little progress across the river.

Then Salva saw the telltale flick of a crocodile's tail as it flopped into the water near the young man. Moments later, the man's head jerked oddly—once, twice. His mouth was open. Perhaps he was screaming, but Salva could not hear him over the din of the crowd and the rain. . . . A moment later, the man was pulled under.

A cloud of red stained the water.

The rain was still pouring down—and now bullets were pouring down as well. The soldiers started shooting into the river, aiming their guns at the people who were trying to get across.

Why? Why are they shooting at us?

Salva had no choice. He jumped into the water and began to swim. A boy next to him grabbed him around the neck and clung to him tightly. Salva was forced under the surface without time to take more than a quick, shallow breath.

Salva struggled—kicking, clawing. *He's holding on to me too hard . . . I can't . . . air . . . no air left . . .*

Suddenly, the boy's grip loosened, and Salva launched himself upward. He threw his head back and took a huge gulp of air. For a few moments he could do nothing but gasp and choke.

When his vision cleared, he saw why the boy had let go: He was floating with his head down, blood streaming from a bullet hole in the back of his neck.

Stunned, Salva realized that being forced under the

water had probably saved his life. But there was no time to marvel over this. More crocodiles were launching themselves off the banks. The rain, the mad current, the bullets, the crocodiles, the welter of arms and legs, the screams, the blood. . . . He had to get across somehow.

Salva did not know how long he was in the water.

It felt like hours.

It felt like years.

When at last the tips of his toes touched mud, he forced his limbs to make swimming motions one last time. He crawled onto the riverbank and collapsed. Then he lay there in the mud, choking and sobbing for breath.

Later, he would learn that at least a thousand people had died trying to cross the river that day, drowned or shot or attacked by crocodiles.

How was it that he was not one of the thousand? Why was he one of the lucky ones?

The walking began again. Walking—but to where?

No one knew anything for sure. Where was Salva supposed to go?

Not home. There is still war everywhere in Sudan.

Not back to Ethiopia. The soldiers would shoot us.

Kenya. There are supposed to be refugee camps in Kenya.

Salva made up his mind. He would walk south, to Kenya. He did not know what he would find once he got there, but it seemed to be his best choice.

Crowds of other boys followed him. Nobody talked about it, but by the end of the first day Salva had become the leader of a group of about fifteen hundred boys. Some were as young as five years old.

Those smallest boys reminded Salva of his brother Kuol. But then he had an astounding thought. *Kuol isn't that age anymore—he is a teenager now!* Salva found that he could only think of his brothers and sisters as they were when he had last seen them, not as they would be now.

They were traveling through a part of Sudan still plagued by war. The fighting and bombing were worst during the day, so Salva decided that the group should hide when the sun shone and do their walking at night.

But in the darkness, it was hard to be sure they were headed in the right direction. Sometimes the boys traveled for days only to realize that they had gone in a huge circle. This happened so many times that Salva lost count. They met other groups of boys, all walking south. Every group had stories of terrible peril: boys who had been hurt or killed by bullets or bombs, attacked by wild animals, or left behind because they were too weak or sick to keep up.

When Salva heard the stories, he thought of Marial. He felt his determination growing, as it had in the days after Uncle's death.

I will get us safely to Kenya, he thought. *No matter how hard it is.*

He organized the group, giving everyone a job: scavenge for food; collect firewood; stand guard while the group slept. Whatever food or water they found was shared equally among all of them. When the smaller boys grew too tired to walk, the older boys took turns carrying them on their backs.

There were times when some of the boys did not want to do their share of the work. Salva would talk to them, encourage them, coax and persuade them. Once in a while he had to speak sternly, or even shout. But he tried not to do this too often.

It was as if Salva's family were helping him, even though they were not there. He remembered how he had looked after his little brother, Kuol. But he also knew what it felt like to have to listen to the older ones, Ariik and Ring. And he could recall the gentleness of his sisters; the strength of his father; the care of his mother.

Most of all, he remembered how Uncle had encouraged him in the desert.

One step at a time . . . one day at a time. Just today—just this day to get through . . .

Salva told himself this every day. He told the boys in the group, too.

And one day at a time, the group made its way to Kenya.

More than twelve hundred boys arrived safely.

It took them a year and a half.

CHAPTER FOURTEEN

Southern Sudan, 2009

For three days, the air around Nya's home was filled with the sound of the drill. On the third afternoon, Nya joined the other children gathered around the drill site. The grownups rose from their work pounding rocks and drifted over, too.

The workers seemed excited. They were moving quickly as their leader called out orders. Then—

WHOOSH!

A spray of water shot high into the air!

This wasn't the water that the workers had been piping *into* the borehole. This was *new* water—water that was coming *out of* the hole!

Everyone cheered at the sight of the water. They all laughed at the sight of the two workers who had been operating the drill. They were drenched, their clothes completely soaked through.

A woman in the crowd began singing a song of celebration. Nya clapped her hands along with all the other children. But as Nya watched the water spraying out of the borehole, she frowned.

The water wasn't clear. It was brown and heavy-looking.
It was full of mud.

Ifo refugee camp, Kenya, 1992–96

Salva was now twenty-two years old. For the past five years
he had been living in refugee camps in northern Kenya:
first at the Kakuma camp, then at Ifo.

Kakuma had been a dreadful place, isolated in the
middle of a dry, windy desert. Tall fences of barbed wire
enclosed the camp; you weren't allowed to leave unless
you were leaving for good. It felt almost like a prison.

Seventy thousand people lived at Kakuma. Some said
it was more, eighty or ninety thousand. There were families who had managed to escape together, but again, as in
Ethiopia, most of the refugees were orphaned boys and
young men.

The local people who lived in the area did not like
having the refugee camp nearby. They would often sneak
in and steal from the refugees. Sometimes fights broke
out, and people were hurt or killed.

After two years of misery at Kakuma, Salva decided to

leave the camp. He had heard of another refugee camp, far to the south and east, where he hoped things would be better.

Once again, Salva and a few other young men walked for months. But when they reached the camp at Ifo, they found that things were no different than at Kakuma. Everyone was always hungry, and there was never enough food. Many were sick or had gotten injured during their long, terrible journeys to reach the camp; the few medical volunteers could not care for everyone who needed help. Salva felt fortunate that at least he was in good health.

He wanted desperately to work—to make a little money that he could use to buy extra food. He even dreamed of saving some money so that one day he could leave the camp and continue his education somehow.

But there was no work. There was nothing to do but wait—wait for the next meal, for news of the world outside the camp. The days were long and empty. They stretched into weeks, then months, then years.

It was hard to keep hope alive when there was so little to feed it.

Michael was an aid worker from a country called Ireland. Salva had met a lot of aid workers. They came and went, staying at the camp for several weeks or, at most, a few months. The aid workers came from many different countries, but they usually spoke English to each other. Few of the refugees spoke English, so communication with the aid workers was often difficult.

But after so many years in the camps, Salva could understand a little English. He even tried to speak it once in a while, and Michael almost always seemed to understand what Salva was trying to say.

One day after the morning meal, Michael spoke to Salva. "You seem interested in learning English," he said. "How'd you like to learn to read?"

The lessons began that very day. Michael wrote down three letters on a small scrap of paper.

"A, B, C," he said, handing the scrap to Salva.

"A, B, C," Salva repeated.

The whole rest of the day, Salva went around saying, "A, B, C," mostly to himself but sometimes aloud, in a quiet voice. He looked at the paper a hundred times and practiced drawing the letters in the dirt with a stick, over and over again.

Salva remembered learning to read Arabic when he was young. The Arabic alphabet had twenty-eight letters; the English, only twenty-six. In English, the letters stayed separate from each other, so it was easy to tell them apart. In Arabic words, the letters were always joined, and a letter might look different depending on what came before or after it.

"Sure, you're doing lovely," Michael said the day Salva learned to write his own name. "You learn fast, because you work so hard."

Salva did not say what he was thinking: that he was working hard because he wanted to learn to read English before Michael left the camp. Salva did not know if any of the other aid workers would take the time to teach him.

"But once in a while it's good to take a break from work. Let's do something a wee bit different for a change. I'm thinking you'll be good at this—you're a tall lad."

So Salva learned two things from Michael: how to read and how to play volleyball.

A rumor was spreading through the camp. It began as a whisper, but soon Salva felt as if it were a roar in his ears. He could think of nothing else.

America.

The United States.

The rumor was that about three thousand boys and

young men from the refugee camps would be chosen to go live in America!

Salva could not believe it. How could it be true? How would they get there? Where would they live? Surely it was impossible. . . .

But as the days went by, the aid workers confirmed the news.

It was all anyone could talk about.

"They only want healthy people. If you are sick, you won't be chosen."

"They won't take you if you have ever been a soldier with the rebels."

"Only orphans are being chosen. If you have any family left, you have to stay here."

Weeks passed, then months. One day a notice was posted at the camp's administration tent. It was a list of names. If your name was on the list, it meant that you had made it to the next step: the interview. After the interview, you might go to America.

Salva's name was not on the list.

Nor was it on the next list, or the one after that.

Many of the boys being chosen were younger than Salva. *Perhaps America doesn't want anyone too old,* he thought.

Each time a list was posted, Salva's heart would pound as he read the names. He tried not to lose hope. At the same time, he tried not to hope too much.

Sometimes he felt he was being torn in two by the hoping and the not hoping.

One windy afternoon, Michael rushed over to Salva's tent.

"Salva! Come quickly! Your name is on the list today!"

Salva leapt to his feet and was running even before his friend had finished speaking. When he drew near the administration tent, he slowed down and tried to catch his breath.

He might be wrong. It might be another person named Salva. I won't look too soon. . . . From far away I might see a name that looks like mine, and I need to be sure.

Salva shouldered his way through the crowd until he was standing in front of the list. He raised his head slowly and began reading through the names.

There it was.

Salva Dut—Rochester, New York.

Salva was going to New York.

He was going to America!

CHAPTER FIFTEEN

Even though the water spraying out of the borehole was brown and muddy, some of the little boys wanted a drink right away. But their mothers held them back. The men kept on working with the drill. Their leader talked to Nya's uncle and father and some of the other village men.

Later, Dep explained things to her. "Don't worry!" he said. "The water is muddy because it is still mixed with the old water that they were using from the pond. They have to drill farther down, to make sure of getting deep enough into the good clean water underground. And then they have to put in the pipes, and make a foundation with the gravel, and then install the pump and pour cement around it. And the cement has to dry."

It would be several more days before they could drink the water, Dep said.

Nya sighed and picked up the big plastic can. Yet another walk to the pond.

❧

The Lost Boys.

That was what they were being called in America—the boys who had lost their homes and families because of the war and had wandered, lost, for weeks or months at a time before reaching the refugee camps.

The aid worker explained this to Salva and the eight other boys he would be traveling with. The woman spoke mostly English. Sometimes she said a word or two in Arabic, but she did not speak that language well. She tried her best to speak slowly, but she had many things to tell them, and Salva worried that he might misunderstand something important.

They rode in a truck from the Ifo refugee camp to a processing center in Nairobi, the capital city of Kenya. Endless forms had to be filled out. Their photos were taken. There was a medical examination. It was all a blur to Salva, for he was too excited to sleep, which made him too tired to grasp everything that was happening.

But there was one clear moment: when he was given new clothes. In the camp, he had worn an old pair of shorts and an even older T-shirt. He had taken as good care of them as he could, but there were holes in the shirt, and the waistband of the shorts was stretched out and threadbare. The camp workers handed out clothing whenever donations came in, but there were never enough clothes for those who needed them.

Now Salva's arms were piled high with new clothes. Underwear, socks, sneakers. A pair of long pants. A T-shirt and a long-sleeved shirt to wear on top of it. And he was to wear *all* these clothes at the same time!

"It's winter in America," the aid worker said.

"Winter?" Salva repeated.

"Yes. Very cold. You will be given more clothes in New York."

More clothes? Salva shook his head. *How can I possibly wear any more clothes?*

Salva could hardly believe his eyes when he boarded the plane in Nairobi. Every person had a seat, and they all had luggage, too. With all those people, hundreds of heavy padded chairs, and all those bags, how would the plane ever get off the ground?

Somehow it did—not like a bird lifting off lightly with a quick flapping of wings, but with shrieks and roars from the engines as the plane lumbered down the long runway, as if it had to try as hard as it could to get into the air.

Once the plane was safely aloft, Salva stared at the scene outside the small window. The world was so big, yet everything in it was so small! Huge forests and deserts became mere patches of green and brown. Cars crawled along the roads like ants in a line. And there were people down there, thousands of them, but he could not see a single one.

"Would you like a drink?"

Salva looked up at the woman in her neat uniform and shook his head to show that he did not understand. She smiled. "Coca-Cola? Orange juice?"

Coca-Cola! Long ago, Salva's father had once brought a few bottles of Coca-Cola back from his trip to the market. Salva's first taste had been startling—all those bubbles jumping around in his mouth! What a rare treat it had been.

"Coca-Cola, thank you," Salva said. And with each sip, he remembered his family passing the bottles from hand to hand, laughing at the tickly bubbles, sharing and laughing together. . . .

The journey to Salva's new home required not one, not two, but *three* planes. The first plane flew from Nairobi to Frankfurt, in a country called Germany. It landed with an alarming thump, then braked so hard that Salva was thrown forward in his seat; the strap across his stomach caught him hard. He took a second plane from Frankfurt to New York City. It, too, landed abruptly, but this time Salva was ready, and he held tightly to the armrests.

In New York City, the aid worker led the boys to different gates. Some would be making the final leg of their trip alone, while others were in groups of two or three. Salva was the only one going to Rochester. The aid worker said that his new family would be waiting for him there.

On the plane to Rochester, most of the passengers were men traveling on their own. But there were some women, too, and a few families—mothers and fathers and children. Most of the people were white; beginning at the airport in Frankfurt, Salva had seen more white people in the last few hours than he had seen before in his whole lifetime.

He tried not to stare, but he couldn't help studying the families closely. Thoughts kept looping through his mind.

What if my new family isn't there? What if they have changed their minds? What if they meet me and don't like me?

Salva took a deep breath. *A step at a time,* he reminded himself. *Just this flight to get through, for now. . . .*

The plane landed at last, its wheels screeching, while Salva gripped the armrests and braced himself for what was to come.

There they were, smiling and waving in the airport lobby—his new family! Chris, the father; Louise, the mother; and four children. Salva would have siblings, just as he had before. He felt his shoulders relax a little on seeing their eager smiles.

Salva said "Hello" and "Thank you" many times, for in his fatigue and confusion, these were the only words he felt sure about. He could not understand what anyone was saying, especially Louise, who spoke so quickly that at first he was not sure she was even speaking English.

And yes, they *did* have more clothes for him!—a big puffy jacket, a hat, a scarf, gloves. He put on the jacket and zipped it up. The sleeves were so bulky that he felt as if he couldn't move his arms properly. He wondered if he looked very foolish now, with his body and arms so fat and his legs so thin. But none of the family laughed at him, and he soon noticed that they were all wearing the same kind of jacket.

The glass doors of the airport terminal slid open. The frigid air hit Salva's face like a slap. Never had he felt such cold before! In the part of Africa where he had lived all his life, the temperature rarely dropped below seventy degrees.

When he inhaled, he thought his lungs would surely freeze solid and stop working. But all around him, people were still walking and talking and moving about. Apparently, it was possible to survive in such cold temperatures, and he now understood the need for the awkward padded jacket.

Salva stood still inside the terminal doors for a few moments. Leaving the airport felt like leaving his old life forever—Sudan, his village, his family. . . .

Tears came to his eyes, perhaps from the cold air blowing in through the open doors. His new family was already outside; they turned and looked back at him.

Salva blinked away the tears and took his first step into a new life in America.

CHAPTER SIXTEEN

Southern Sudan, 2009

After the excitement of seeing that first spray of water, the villagers went back to work. Several men gathered in front of Nya's house. They had tools with them, hoes and spades and scythes.

Her father went out to meet them. The men walked together to a spot beyond the second big tree and began clearing the land.

Nya watched them for a few moments. Her father saw her and waved. She put the plastic can down and ran over to him.

"Papa, what are you doing?"

"Clearing the land here. Getting ready to build."

"To build what?"

Nya's father smiled. "Can't you guess?"

Rochester, New York, 1996–2003

Salva had been in Rochester for nearly a month and still had not seen a single dirt road. Unlike southern Sudan, it seemed that here in America every road was paved. At times, the cars whizzed by so fast, he was amazed that anyone on foot could cross safely. His new father, Chris, told him that dirt roads did exist out in the countryside, but there were none in Salva's new neighborhood.

All the buildings had electricity. There were white people everywhere. Snow fell from the sky for hours at a time and then stayed on the ground for days. Sometimes it would start to melt during the day, but before it all disappeared, more snow would fall. Salva's new mother, Louise, told him it would probably be April—three more months— before the snow went away completely.

The first several weeks of Salva's new life were so bewildering that he was grateful for his studies. His lessons, especially English, gave him something to concentrate on, a way to block out the confusion for an hour or two at a time.

His new family helped, too. All of them were kind to him, patiently explaining the millions of things he had to learn.

It had taken four days for Salva to travel from the Ifo refugee camp to his new home in New York. There were times when he could hardly believe he was still on the same planet.

Now that Salva was learning more than a few simple words, he found the English language quite confusing. Like the letters "o-u-g-h." Rough . . . though . . . fought . . . through . . . bough—the same letters were pronounced so many different ways! Or how a word had to be changed depending on the sentence. You said "chickens" when you meant the living birds that walked and squawked and laid eggs, but it was "chicken"—with no "s"—when it was on your plate ready to be eaten: "We're having chicken for dinner." That was correct, even if you had cooked a hundred chickens.

Sometimes he wondered if he would ever be able to speak and read English well. But slowly, with hours of hard work over the months and years, his English improved. Remembering Michael, Salva also joined a volleyball team. It was fun playing volleyball, just as it had been at the camp. Setting and spiking the ball were the same in any language.

Salva had been in Rochester for more than six years now. He was going to college and had decided to study business. He had a vague idea that he would like to return to Sudan someday, to help the people who lived there.

Sometimes that seemed like an impossible notion. In his homeland there was so much war and destruction, poverty, disease, and starvation—so many problems that had not been solved by governments, or rich people, or big aid organizations. What could he possibly do to help? Salva thought about this question a lot, but no answer came to him.

One evening at the end of a long day of study, Salva sat down at the family computer and opened his e-mail. He was surprised to see a message from a cousin of his—someone he barely knew. The cousin was working for a relief agency in Zimbabwe.

Salva clicked open the message. His eyes read the words, but at first his brain could not comprehend them.

"... United Nations clinic ... your father ... stomach surgery ..."

Salva read the words again and again. Then he jumped to his feet and ran through the house to find Chris and Louise.

"My father!" he shouted. "They have found my father!"

After several exchanges of e-mails, Salva learned that the cousin had not actually seen or spoken to his father. The clinic where his father was recovering was in a remote part of southern Sudan. There was no telephone or mail service—no way of communicating with the clinic staff. The staff kept lists of all the patients they treated. These lists were submitted to the United Nations' aid agencies. Salva's cousin worked for one of the agencies, and he had seen the name of Salva's father on a list.

Salva immediately began planning to travel to Sudan. But with the war still raging, it was very difficult to make the arrangements. He had to get permits, fill out dozens of forms, and organize plane flights and car transport in a region where there were no airports or roads.

Salva, and Chris and Louise as well, spent hours on the phone to various agencies and offices. It took not days or weeks but *months* before all the plans were in place. And there was no way to get a message to the hospital. At times, Salva felt almost frantic at the delays and frustrations. *What if my father leaves the hospital without telling anyone where he is going? What if I get there too late? I will never be able to find him again. . . .*

At last, all the forms were filled out, and all the paperwork was in order. Salva flew in a jet to New York City, another one to Amsterdam, and a third to Kampala in Uganda. In Kampala, it took him two days to get through customs and immigration before he could board a smaller plane to go to Juba, in southern Sudan. Then he rode in a jeep on dusty dirt roads into the bush.

How familiar everything was and yet how different! The unpaved roads, the scrubby bushes and trees, the huts roofed with sticks bound together—everything was just as Salva remembered it, as if he had left only yesterday. At the same time, the memories of his life in Sudan were very distant. How could memories feel so close and so far away at the same time?

After many hours of jolting and bumping along the roads in the jeep—after nearly a week of exhausting travel—Salva entered the shanty that served as a recovery room at the makeshift hospital. A white woman stood to greet him.

"Hello," he said. "I am looking for a patient named Mawien Dut Ariik."

CHAPTER SEVENTEEN

"What do you think we are building here?" Nya's father asked, smiling.

"A house?" Nya guessed. "Or a barn?"

Her father shook his head. "Something better," he said. "A school."

Nya's eyes widened. The nearest school was half a day's walk from their home. Nya knew this because Dep had wanted to go there. But it was too far.

"A school?" she echoed.

"Yes," he replied. "With the well here, no one will have to go to the pond anymore. So all the children will be able to go to school."

Nya stared at her father. Her mouth opened, but no words came out. When at last she was able to speak, it was only in a whisper. "*All* the children, Papa? The girls, too?"

Her father's smile grew broader. "Yes, Nya. Girls, too," he said. "Now, go and fetch water for us." And he returned to his work scything the long grass.

Nya went back and picked up the plastic can. She felt as if she were flying.

School! She would learn to read and write!

Sudan and Rochester, New York, 2003–2007

🐾

Salva stood at the foot of one of the beds in the crowded clinic.

"Hello," he said.

"Hello," the patient replied politely.

"I have come to visit you," Salva said.

"To visit me?" The man frowned. "But who are you?"

"You are Mawien Dut Ariik, aren't you?"

"Yes, that is my name."

Salva smiled, his insides trembling. Even though his father looked older now, Salva had recognized him right away. But it was as if his eyes needed help from his ears—he needed to hear his father's words to believe he was real.

"I am your son. I am Salva."

The man looked at Salva and shook his head. "No," he said. "It is not possible."

"Yes," Salva said. "It's me, Father." He moved to the side of the bed.

Mawien Dut reached out and touched the arm of this tall stranger beside him. "Salva?" he whispered. "Can it really be you?"

Salva waited. Mawien Dut stared for a long moment. Then he cried out, "Salva! My son, my son!"

His body shaking with sobs of joy, he reached up to hug Salva tightly.

It had been almost nineteen years since they had last seen each other.

Mawien Dut sprinkled water on his son's head, the Dinka way of blessing someone who was lost and is found again.

"Everyone was sure you were dead," Mawien Dut said. "The village wanted to kill a cow for you."

That was how Salva's people mourned the death of a loved one.

"I would not let them," his father said. "I never gave up hope that you were still alive somewhere."

"And . . . and my mother?" Salva asked, barely daring to hope.

His father smiled. "She is back in the village."

Salva wanted to laugh and cry at the same time. "I must see her!"

But his father shook his head. "There is still war near Loun-Ariik, my son. If you went there, both sides would try to force you to fight with them. You must not go."

There was so much more to talk about. His father told Salva that his sisters were with his mother. But of his three brothers, only Ring had survived the war. Ariik, the oldest, and Kuol, the youngest, were both dead.

Little Kuol . . . Salva closed his eyes for a few moments, trying to picture his brothers through a haze of time and grief.

He learned more about his father's illness. Years of drinking contaminated water had left Mawien Dut's entire digestive system riddled with guinea worms. Sick and weak, he had walked almost three hundred miles to come to this clinic, and was barely alive by the time he finally arrived.

Salva and his father had several days together. But all too soon, it was time for Salva to return to America. His father would be leaving the clinic shortly as well. The surgery he had undergone had been successful, and he would soon be strong enough to make the long walk home.

"I will come to the village," Salva promised, "as soon as it is safe."

"We will be there waiting for you," his father promised in turn.

Salva pressed his face tightly to his father's as they hugged goodbye, their tears flowing and blending together.

On the plane back to the United States, Salva replayed in his mind every moment of his visit with his father. He felt again the coolness on his brow when his father had sprinkled the water blessing on him.

And an idea came to him—an idea of what he might be able to do to help the people of Sudan.

Could he do it? It would take so much work! Perhaps it would be too difficult. But how would he know unless he tried?

Back in Rochester, Salva began working on his idea. There were, it seemed, a million problems to be solved. He needed a lot of help. Chris and Louise gave him many suggestions. Scott, a friend of theirs, was an expert in setting up projects like the one Salva had in mind. He and Salva worked together for hours and days . . . which grew into weeks and months.

Along the way, Salva met other people who wanted to help. He was grateful to all of them. But even with their help, it was much more work than he had imagined.

Salva had to raise money for the project. And there was only one way to do this: He would have to talk to people and ask them to give money.

The first time Salva spoke in front of an audience was in a school cafeteria. About a hundred people had come to hear him. There was a microphone at the front of the room. Salva's knees were shaking as he walked to the mike. He knew that his English was still not very good. What if he made mistakes in pronunciation? What if the audience couldn't understand him?

But he had to do it. If he didn't talk about the project, no one would learn about it. No one would donate money, and he would never be able to make it work.

Salva spoke into the microphone. "H-h-hello," he said.

At that moment, something went wrong with the sound system. The speakers behind him let out a dreadful screech. Salva jumped and almost dropped the mike.

His hands trembling, he looked out at the audience. People were smiling or chuckling; a few of the children were holding their ears. They all looked very friendly, and seeing the children made him remember: It was not the first time he had spoken in front of a large group of people.

Years before, when he was leading those boys on their walk from the Ethiopian refugee camp to the one in Kenya, he had called a meeting every morning and evening. The boys would line up facing him and he would talk to them about their plans.

All those eyes looking at him . . . but every face interested in what he had to say. It was the same here. The audience had come to the school cafeteria because they wanted to hear him. Thinking of that made him feel a little better, and he spoke into the mike again.

"Hello," he repeated, and this time only his own voice came from the speakers. He smiled in relief and went on. "I am here to talk to you about a project for southern Sudan."

A year passed, then two . . . then three. Salva spoke to hundreds of people—in churches, at civic organizations, in schools. Would he ever be able to turn his idea into reality? Whenever he found himself losing hope, Salva would take a deep breath and think of his uncle's words.

A *step at a time.*

One problem at a time—just figure out this one problem.

Day by day, solving one problem at a time, Salva moved toward his goal.

CHAPTER EIGHTEEN

Nya waited her turn in line. She was holding a plastic bottle.

The well was finally finished. The gravel had been put down to make a foundation, the pump had been installed, and the cement had been poured and left to dry.

Before the pump was used for the first time, the villagers all gathered around. The leader of the workers brought out a big sign made of blue canvas. The canvas had writing on it. The writing was in English, but the leader spoke to Nya's uncle, and Uncle told everyone what the sign said.

"'In honor of Elm Street School,'" Uncle said. "This is the name of a school in America. The students at the school raised the money for this well to be dug."

Uncle held up one end of the sign. The workers' leader held up the other end. Everyone else stood around it, and one of the workers took their picture. The picture would be sent to the American school so that the students there could see the well and the people who were now using it.

Then the villagers all got in line to wait their turn for water from the new well.

When Nya reached the head of the line, she smiled shyly at her uncle, who paused in his work for a moment to smile back at her. Then he began moving the pump handle. Up and down, up and down . . .

A stream of water flowed from the mouth of the pump.

Nya held her bottle underneath the pump mouth. The bottle filled up quickly.

She stepped aside to let the next person fill a bottle. Then she drank.

The water was delicious. It wasn't warm or muddy, like the water from the pond. It was cool and clear.

Nya stopped drinking and held up the bottle so she could look at it. Funny that something without any color at all could look so nice.

She drank a few more sips, then glanced around.

Everyone had a bottle or a cup. They were drinking that lovely water, or waiting in line for more, or talking and laughing. It was a celebration.

An old granddad standing not far from Nya shook his head. In a loud voice, he said, "This is where we used to gather for our bonfire celebrations. I have been sitting on this ground my whole life. And all those years I never knew that I was sitting on top of this good water!"

Everyone around him laughed. Nya laughed, too.

In a few more days, the school would be finished. Nya and Dep and Akeer would all go to school, along with the other children. Next year there would be a marketplace where the villagers could sell and buy vegetables and chickens and other goods. There was even talk of a clinic someday—a medical clinic, so they wouldn't have to walk so far to get help, as they had to when Akeer was ill.

It was the well that was bringing the village all these good things.

But the well was not for their use alone. People would come from miles around to fetch the good clean water. Nya knew from listening to the grownups that the crew leader had made many arrangements concerning the well. No one was ever to be refused water. Some of the villagers would be responsible for maintaining the well. They would be busy with this new work, so the entire village was to help them with their crops and cattle. Other villagers, including Nya's uncle, would resolve any disputes that arose.

The well would change their lives in many ways.

I will never again have to walk to the pond for water, Nya thought.

She wandered around a little, sipping at her cool, fresh

drink. Then she caught sight of the crew leader. He was standing by himself, leaning against one of the trucks and watching her uncle work the pump.

Dep saw her looking at the man.

"That man, the boss of the workers," Dep said. "You know he is Dinka?"

Nya looked at Dep in astonishment.

The Dinka and the Nuer did not look very different physically. You had to look at the scar patterns on people's faces to tell the tribes apart—Dinka scar patterns were different from those of the Nuer.

But the crew leader had no scars on his face. Nya had heard some of the teenage boys talking about that—wondering why he had no scars when clearly he was a grown man. The leader's assistant was Nuer. So were most of the crew—they all had Nuer scars. Nya hadn't thought about it much, but she realized now she had always assumed that the leader was Nuer, too.

The Dinka and the Nuer were enemies—had been for hundreds of years.

"Why would a Dinka bring water to us?" she wondered aloud.

"I heard Uncle and Father talking about him," Dep said.

"He has drilled many wells for his own people. This year he decided to drill for the Nuer as well."

Dep had not really answered Nya's question. *He probably doesn't know the answer,* she thought. But now Nya felt there was something she had to do.

She walked over to where the man was standing. He didn't notice her at first, so she waited quietly.

Then he saw her. "Hello," he said.

Shyness flooded through Nya. For a moment, she didn't think she would be able to speak. She looked down at the ground, then at the stream of water still flowing from the pump mouth.

And she found her voice. "Thank you," she said, and looked up at him bravely. "Thank you for bringing the water."

The man smiled. "What is your name?" he asked.

"I am Nya."

"I am happy to meet you, Nya," he said. "My name is Salva."

This book is based on the true story of my life. I hope that because of the book more people will learn about the Lost Boys and the country of Sudan.

I was born in a small village called Loun-Ariik, in Tonj County, southern Sudan. And just as it says in the book, I stayed in refugee camps in Ethiopia and Kenya for many years before I came to America.

I am thankful to a great many people. The United Nations and the International Red Cross supported my life when I was in danger of starvation. The Moore family, St. Paul Episcopal Church, and the community of Rochester, New York, welcomed me to the United States. I am also grateful for the education I have received, especially at Monroe Community College.

And deepest gratitude to the people who have helped me with my project, Water for Sudan, Inc.—the schools, churches, civic organizations, and individuals all over the country. Special thanks to the Board of Water for Sudan, and to the Rotary Clubs that have worked closely with me. My dreams of helping the people back home in Sudan are beginning to come true.

I overcame all the difficult situations of my past because of the hope and perseverance that I had. I would have not made it without these two things. To young people, I would like to say: Stay calm when things are hard or not going right with you. You will get through it when you persevere instead of quitting. Quitting leads to much less happiness in life than perseverance and hope.

Salva Dut
Rochester, New York

2010

Some of the details in this story have been fictionalized, but the major events depicted are based on Salva's own experiences. I read his written accounts and interviewed him for many hours. I also read other books and accounts by and about Lost Boys. For Nya's part of the story, I was able to interview travelers who have seen the water wells being drilled in villages like hers; I also benefited from examining their video footage and photographs.

Known as the Second Sudanese Civil War, the conflict that is depicted in this book began in 1983. Many factions were involved and numerous changes in leadership took place over the duration of the war, but in essence, the opposing sides were the Muslim-dominated government in the north and the non-Muslim coalition in the south. Besides religion, economic strife was an important factor, as the country's reserves of oil are located in the south.

Millions of people were killed, imprisoned, tortured, kidnapped, or enslaved; millions more were permanently displaced, unable to return to their homes. Among those displaced were hundreds of thousands of so-called Lost Boys like Salva, who walked in desperation through southern Sudan, Ethiopia, and Kenya in search of safe haven.

Many of the Lost Boys who were able to return home after the war found that their families had vanished. Others languished in refugee camps like those Salva lived in. Some were eventually reunited with their loved ones, often after decades apart.

In 2002, nearly twenty years after the war began, the United States government passed the Sudan Peace Act, officially accusing the Sudanese government of genocide in the deaths of more than two million people. Three years later, a peace accord was signed between the north and south. The south was granted autonomy—the ability to govern itself—for six years. In 2011, a referendum took place in which the citizens of southern Sudan voted to secede, gaining their independence from the north. Unrest over South Sudan's oil and its political leadership have roiled its infancy as the world's newest nation.

The war in Darfur, in the western part of Sudan, is a separate conflict, not covered by the peace accord. As of this writing, that war is still being fought between factions who identify themselves as Arabic and those who consider themselves African. The two wars, combined with several years of severe drought, have brought untold suffering to the people of Sudan.

Salva has seen his family in Sudan twice more since the events of this story, including a moving reunion with his cousins, the children of Uncle Jewiir. And amazingly, seven of the Lost Boys who walked with Salva from Ethiopia to Kenya met up with him again when they were relocated to the Rochester, New York, area.

As of spring 2014, Salva Dut's nonprofit organization Water for South Sudan has drilled more than 250 wells in southern Sudan for Dinka and Nuer communities, supplying fresh water for hundreds of thousands of people. The very first well was drilled in Salva's home village of Loun-Ariik. Salva moved to South Sudan in 2011 and now lives there. You can learn more about the organization's work at www.waterforsouthsudan.org.

I first met Salva several years ago when my husband and I learned about Water for South Sudan. In 2008 and 2015, my husband traveled to South Sudan to see Salva's work. I am grateful for his help in answering my endless questions: This story could not have been written without him.

My family and I feel very fortunate to count Salva as a friend. It has truly been an honor for me to write this book with him.

Addendum, 2015

A Long Walk to Water was first published in 2010. Since then, to my surprise and joy, many readers who have learned about Salva Dut's amazing story have been inspired to action. Teachers, librarians, school administrators, parents, and most especially students have raised hundreds of thousands of dollars for Salva's nonprofit organization, Water for South Sudan.

The most popular fundraiser is a walk for water. Some schools arrange for students to carry heavy jugs of water while walking, just like Nya does in the book. Other schools take the H_2O challenge, drinking only water for a period of time and donating the cost of other beverages such as soda.

A "wishing well" in the school lobby or cafeteria to receive donations of spare change; paper drops of water sponsored and displayed on a wall; individual students requesting contributions in lieu of birthday or bar/bat mitzvah gifts: We're so impressed at the multitude of fun, creative, and effective fundraising strategies we've heard about.

Salva and I want to sincerely thank you all. Because of your efforts, hundreds of water wells have been drilled, and many of them bear the names of the schools whose donations enabled their construction. Your hard work is literally saving people's lives, every single day.

If you would like to join this lifesaving effort, please visit the website waterforsouthsudan.org. You'll find up-to-date reports on Salva's work, lots of photos and videos, and information on current campaigns, as well as more ideas for fundraising.

Keep reading . . . and walk the walk!

—Linda Sue Park and Salva Dut

Acknowledgments

Sincere thanks to:

Chris and Louise Moore and their children,

Salva's American family;

John Turner, Nancy Frank,

and the other members of the board of

Water for South Sudan;

Jeffrey Mead for the opportunity

to view photos and video footage;

and Linda Wright and Sue Kassirer

of Breakfast Serials, Inc.

Ginger Knowlton, David Barbor,

and everyone at Curtis Brown, Ltd.

And Dinah Stevenson,

for nudges both gentle and firm,

and always in the right direction.